Anonymous

Fiftieth Anniversary Celebration of the Mercantile Library Association

Anatiposi

Anonymous

Fiftieth Anniversary Celebration of the Mercantile Library Association

Reprint of the original, first published in 1871.

1st Edition 2023 | ISBN: 978-3-38217-418-7

Anatiposi Verlag is an imprint of Outlook Verlagsgesellschaft mbH.

Verlag (Publisher): Outlook Verlag GmbH, Zeilweg 44, 60439 Frankfurt, Deutschland
Vertretungsberechtigt (Authorized to represent): E. Roepke, Zeilweg 44, 60439 Frankfurt, Deutschland
Druck (Print): Books on Demand GmbH, In de Tarpen 42, 22848 Norderstedt, Deutschland

FIFTIETH ANNIVERSARY

CELEBRATION

OF THE

Mercantile Library Association

OF THE

CITY OF NEW-YORK,

AT THE

ACADEMY OF MUSIC, NOV. 9th, 1870.

AND THE

Fifth Anniversary Celebration

OF THE

EX-OFFICERS' UNION,

AT

DELMONICO'S, NOV. 10th, 1870.

NEW-YORK:

GEORGE F. NESBITT & CO., PRINTERS AND STATIONERS,

Corner of Pearl and Pine Streets.

1871.

FIFTIETH ANNIVERSARY

CELEBRATION

OF THE

Mercantile Library Association

OF THE

CITY OF NEW-YORK,

AT THE

ACADEMY OF MUSIC, NOV. 9th, 1870.

AND THE

Fifth Anniversary Celebration

OF THE

EX-OFFICERS' UNION,

AT

DELMONICO'S, NOV. 10th, 1870.

NEW-YORK:

GEORGE F. NESBITT & CO., PRINTERS AND STATIONERS,
Corner of Pearl and Pine Streets.

1871.

Presidents of the Association

FROM ITS ORGANIZATION.

1820-23..*LUCIUS BULL.*

1823-24..*CORNELIUS SAVAGE.*

1824-26..*BENJAMIN I. SEWARD.*

1827-31..*R. B. BROWN.*

1832-34..*JOHN W. STEBBINS.*

1834-35..*R. R. BOYD.*

1836-37..*CHARLES ROLFE.*

1838.....*EDMUND COFFIN.*

1839.....*JOHN S. WINTHROP.*

1839.....*ELIJAH WARD.*

1840.....*AUGUSTUS E. SILLIMAN.*

1841.....*HECTOR MORISON,*

1842.....*JOHN T. ROLLINS.*

1843.....*LEWIS McMULLEN.*

1843.....*RICHARD BURLEW.*

1844-45..*CHARLES E. MILNOR.*

1846-47..*CORNELIUS L. EVERETT.*

1848.....*THOMAS W. GROSER.*

1849.....*ISAAC H. BAILEY.*

1850.....*THOMAS J. BAYAUD.*

1851.....*HENRY A. OAKLEY.*

1852.....*GEORGE PECKHAM.*

1853.....*WILLARD L. FELT.*

1854.....*DANIEL F. APPLETON.*

1855.....*D. REYNOLDS BUDD.*

1855-56..*GEORGE C. WOOD.*

1856-57..*JOHN CRERAR.*

1857-58..*ROWLAND H. TIMPSON.*

1857-58..*ALEXANDER P. FISKE.*

1858-59..*E. BOUDINOT SERVOSS.*

1859-60..*RICHARD A. BACHIA.*

1860-61..*CHAS. E. KING SHERMAN.*

1861-62..*CHARLES F. ALLEN.*

1862-63..*CHARLES OSGOOD.*

1863-64..*CHARLES H. SWORDS.*

1864-65..*THEODORE H. VULTEE.*

1865-66..*ROBERT WALKER IRWIN.*

1866-67..*AARON C. ALLEN.*

1867-68..*ALEXANDER RHIND.*

1868-69..*CHARLES F. ALLEN.*

1869-70..*M. C. D. BORDEN.*

Officers and Members of the Board of Direction

AND

OFFICERS

OF THE

MERCANTILE LIBRARY ASSOCIATION FOR 1870-71.

President,
M. C. D. BORDEN.

Vice-President,
W. T. PEOPLES.

Corresponding Secretary,	*Recording Secretary,*
EDWARD HASLER.	**SAMUEL PUTNAM.**

Treasurer,
GEORGE B. MILLS.

Directors of the First Class, to hold office for One Year,

M. C. D. BORDEN,	N. H. MYRICK,
EDWARD HASLER,	GEO. B. MILLS.

Directors of the Second Class, to hold office for Two Years,

W. T. PEOPLES,	A. W. SHERMAN,
SAMUEL PUTNAM,	J. C. CURRIE.

Directors of the Third Class, to hold office for Three Years,

CHARLES F. ALLEN,	ASHER S. MILLS,
W. A. SHERMAN,	JNO. NICKINSON.

Librarian,
A. M. PALMER.

Assistant Librarian,
GEORGE COOPE.

FIFTIETH
ANNIVERSARY CELEBRATION.

THE Fiftieth Anniversary of the organization of the Mercantile Library Association of the City of New-York, was celebrated in the Academy of Music, on the evening of Wednesday, November 9th, 1870. A very large and brilliant audience was in attendance. The President of the Association, Mr. M. C. D. Borden, occupied the chair; Wilson G. Hunt, Esq., David Dudley Field, Esq., Hon. A. Oakey Hall, William Cullen Bryant, Esq., Hon. Wm. E. Dodge, Cyrus W. Field, Esq., Rev. H. C. Potter, D.D., Rev. Stephen H. Tyng, D.D., Edmund Coffin, Esq., Thomas H. Faile, Esq., Hon. John Cochrane, and many other prominent gentlemen occupied seats upon the stage. The music was furnished by Grafulla's Seventh Regiment Band. The exercises were opened with prayer by Rev. Stephen H. Tyng, D.D.; and the President then delivered the following

OPENING ADDRESS:

LADIES AND GENTLEMEN :—

In a little room in Wall Street, just fifty years ago to-night, there met together a small company of men, identified as merchants' clerks. Assembled at the call of a single gentleman, without any well-defined plan and with no conception of an enterprise that should outlive themselves, this little body of clerks, then and there, gave form to a project which appears to-day as the most extensive and most useful existing institution of its kind. On the 12th of February following, in an upper room of the building known as 49 Fulton Street, our Association was formally introduced to existence by the deposit for circulation of seven hundred volumes, with a total membership of 150 subscribers. Such was our birth as an Association. The first few years of life were uneventful, save in the obstacles and difficulties which inevitably attach to the earlier stages of all human undertakings, and which, in our experience, seemed to prevail in exceptional force.

In point of fact, the five years introductory to our career were in no proper sense a question of *progress*. They were simply and singly a hardly contested struggle for *existence*. Fortunately for us—more happily for society—the first and greatest crisis was safely passed; the period of convalescence began to assert itself, and in 1826, in the month of June, the Library was moved to more eligible and commodious rooms, in the building then owned and occupied by the Harper Bros., in Cliff Street. Here a new feature was added in the form of a Reading Room, unpretentious enough with its complement of four weekly papers and seven magazines; but, nevertheless, a valued and valuable accession. From this date—1826—really begins the progress of the organization. Books accumulate more certainly; papers and magazines increase more sensibly; members, the support and sustenance of the enterprise, multiply with encouraging rapidity, and a few years later on, the merchants of New-York contribute with a generous willingness to place the Library in a building of its own. This was the first Clinton Hall, completed and formally dedicated to our service in November of 1830; built for us; exclusively appropriated to our use; but providently held in trust by a Board of Trustees, composed of older and more experienced men, elected by and representing the subscribers to the building; a duly organized body under the name of the Clinton Hall Association. This relation of the two Associations, which

differ after all in name alone and are identical in purpose,
exists to the present day, and will continue for all time in
the interests of the beneficent cause they together represent.
Firmly established now and steadily progressive, we pass on
to the next and grandest move of all, in 1850, to the Clinton
Hall of to-day, far from its original site, with a membership
of more than 3,000 merchants' clerks, and a store of not less
than 30,000 books.

Such, very briefly, was the Mercantile Library twenty
years ago.   Do you ask what it is to-day ? It has the same
house, which it has outgrown ; it has the same garments,
which it has outworn ; it is the assured and resistless growth
supplanting the small and uncertain seed ; it holds a capital
of one hundred and twenty thousand books, to which it is
adding at the rate of ten per cent. a year ; it has a reading
room which affords to its patrons, access at will, to more
than four hundred newspapers and magazines ; its roll of
members stretches over a list of no less than eleven thousand names, for whose benefit it boasts an income of sixty
thousand dollars a year ; it scatters among its readers an
average of eight hundred volumes a day ; it circulates two
hundred and fifty thousand books a year; it gives more for
less than any Library in the world ; it is the community's
friend—one of those silent but irresistible agencies by which
society is informed and refined ; it is the city's university.
Give it all honor for the good it has done, and your honest
God-speed for the good it has yet to do.   [Applause.]   But
I try your patience too far.

You remember that Mr. Calhoun on one occasion so far
abused his privilege of discussion as to provoke from Mr.
Webster a most sharp and cutting retort—"The honorable
member has made an expedition into regions as remote
from the subject of this debate as the orb of Jupiter from
that of our earth."   And I am reminded that I am as widely
distant from the object that induces your presence as my

indifferent utterance from the rich entertainment of eloquence and speech to which I am presently to invite you.

As the result of circumstances, over which we unfortunately have no control, it has been found necessary to vary somewhat the promised programme of the evening, and I now have the pleasure of presenting to you a gentleman whose name is known and honored by every American audience, as his influence is daily felt by every citizen of the Metropolis who reads, the Nestor of the American Press, Mr. Wm. Cullen Bryant.   [Long continued applause.]

Address of WILLIAM CULLEN BRYANT.

LADIES AND GENTLEMEN :—

I esteem myself highly fortunate in being able to congratulate the members of the Mercantile Library Association on having reached the fiftieth anniversary of their life. Forty-five years ago, when I first came to live in the City of New-York, that Institution was in the early infancy of which your President has just given an interesting account. I remember, very well, that the public-spirited young gentlemen by whom it was founded, expected much from it in the future.   They hoped, and the hope was not vain, that it would greatly aid in forming the minds of the younger part of the mercantile class to liberal tastes and to generous views of their duty to their country and to mankind, and that it would be in some measure a safeguard against the temptations which beset young men in a populous city. Those who then sat by its cradle, if they survive, are now aged men ; those whose birth was coeval with its origin are men of mature age, who have passed the zenith of life ; the books which were collected in its first year, to form the beginning of what is now a flourishing library, belong to the literature of a past generation.   Yet, in founding this Institution, the men of that day left a noble legacy to future

times. While other institutions have risen and fallen, it
has continued to grow and to extend its beneficial influences
with the growth of our city; not, indeed, in the same proportion, but steadily and with a sure advance, till now its
prosperity and duration seem almost beyond the reach of
accident. I learn that there is no Library in the country
which increases so fast as that which belongs to this Association, and that within the last ten years it has more than
doubled the number of its volumes. If it proceeds at this
rate it will eventually have a library which will command
the admiration of the world and become the pride of our
country. [Applause.]

In the years yet to come, far in the depths of the future,
the young men who search among the old books of the
library will say to each other: "See with what reading our
ancestors entertained themselves many centuries since, and
how the language has changed since that time! We can
laugh yet at the humor of Irving, in spite of the antiquated
diction. What a fiery spirit animates the quaint sentences of
the old novelist Cooper! In these verses of Longfellow we
still perceive the sweetness of the numbers and the pathos of
the thoughts, and wonder not that the maidens of that distant age wept over the pages of Evangeline. Here," they
will add, "are the scientific works of that distant age.
Clever men were these ancestors of ours; diligent inquirers;
fortunate discoverers of scientific truth, but how far in its
attainment below the height which we have since reached!"

What I have just now imagined, supposes our flourishing
library to escape destruction by war and by casual fire.
Ah, my friends, never may the fate of unhappy Strasburg
be ours! to lie for weeks under a hail storm of iron and a
rain of fire, showered from the engines of destruction,
which Milton properly makes the guilty invention of the
sinning angels, and doomed to see her library, rich with the
priceless treasures of past centuries, suddenly turned to

ashes. But whatever may be the fate of our library, the Association itself is not so easily destroyed. If the Library perish, the same spirit which founded it first, will restore it so far as restoration is possible. The Association, I venture to predict, will subsist till this great mart of commerce shall be a mart no longer; till the mercantile class shall have disappeared from the spot where it stands, and New-York shall have dwindled to a fishing town.

But will this ever be? Will our great city share the fate of Tyre and Sidon, whose merchants were princes, and which are now but Arab villages, with a few caiques and here and there a felucca moored in their clear but shallow waters, choked with the ruins of palaces? Will she become like Carthage, once mistress of flourishing colonies, but now a desert; like Corinth, once the seat of a vast commerce—opulent, luxurious, magnificent Corinth—now a mere cluster of houses overlooked by a dismantled and mouldering citadel?

Or, to come down to later times, will this city decay like Amsterdam, the mother of New-York, and once the centre of the world's commerce? Or like Genoa, surnamed the proud, and Venice, once the mistress of the Adriatic—cities which after having successively wielded the commerce of the East, and made Italian the language of commerce in all the ports of the Levant, have long since ceased to hold a place among the great marts of the world?

I answer that none of these cities had the same firm and durable basis of commercial prosperity as our New-York. It was their enterprise in opening channels of trade; it was their conquests and colonies which gave them their temporary prosperity. They had no broad, well peopled region around them, under the same government with themselves, whose superabundant products it was their office to exchange with other countries. Their prosperity was built on narrow foundations, and it fell. Our circumstances are different.

Here is a republic of vast extent, stretching from the sea which bathes the western coast of Europe to that which washes the eastern shore of Asia—a region of fertile plains, rich valleys, noble forests, mountains big with mines, water-courses whose sands are gold, mighty rivers, railways going forth from our great cities to every point of the compass, and covering an immense territory with their intersections, and not a hindrance to commerce between city and city or between sea and sea, or on our great rivers, or on the borders of the States forming our confederation. This mighty region, alive with an energetic population, is flanked with seaports, through which the products sent by us to other countries *must* pass, and through which the merchandise sent us in exchange *must* be received. They are therefore an indispensable part of our national economy. Their prosperity is necessary, inevitable, and will endure while our political institution remains as it now is. [Applause.]

But if it should come to pass that this fortunate order of things is broken up, if this great republic should fall to pieces and become divided into a group of independent commonwealths, and if an illiberal legislation should obstruct the channels of trade now so fortunately open over all our vast territory, there are none of our marts of exchange for whose future prosperity I could answer. Some would fall into a slow decay, some pass into a rapid decline; some would become like Ascalon on the coast of Palestine, once a harbor crowded with shipping, but when I saw it, a desolate spot, where the sea-sand had drifted upon the foundations of temples and palaces, invaded the harvest fields, and moving before the wind, had entered the olive groves and piled itself among them to the tops of the trees.

Our security from such unhappy results will, in a good degree, lie in such institutions as this, and in other means of a like character, the object of which is to diffuse knowledge, to open men's eyes to their true interests, and accustom them to large and generous views of the relations of communities to each other and to the world at large. For this reason let us hope for the permanent and increasing prosperity of the Mercantile Library Association. [Great applause.]

The President.—The gentleman whose name is first on the programme in your hands, we had confidently expected to be here, and not until yesterday, at a late hour, did we receive any indication to the contrary. Then came a telegram announcing the impossibility of his coming, over the signature of the Hon. Roscoe Conkling.

Mr. Maretzek, who perhaps, has disappointed a New-York audience more frequently than any other individual, has had the happy faculty of acquitting himself by pleading the illness of the favorite absentee, invariably fortifying his position by the strong armor of professional assertion and doctor's certificate. While we have no positive information of the fact, we are nevertheless justified in supposing that no lesser reason can excuse an absence so inopportune; and, without at this particular time, attempting *to give a name to the disease*, we are forced to the conclusion that the Hon. Senator is seriously sick. [Laughter and great applause.]

The epidemic, however, is wide spread. The Governor of your Commonwealth, no longer ago than on Monday morning, gave me in person the assurance of his presence here to-night, and I hold in my hand unimpeachable evidence of his good will and faith in giving the promise. I have also conclusive evidence for supposing that the Governor has been really ill, far too unwell to risk the exposure that would necessarily attach to his coming out on a night to be remembered for the violence of its storm. I crave the pardon of His Excellency for saying that I think he is ess to be pitied for his unfortunate indisposition than the audience which is thereby deprived of the anticipated pleasure of hearing a thoroughly good speech. But the chapter of difficulties does not end here. [Laughter.] I have to assure you, upon my word of honor, that until two o'clock this very afternoon, we had the positive assurance that the Hon Wm. M. Evarts would speak here to-night. Then came a telegram, bidding our Ex-Attorney-General to Washington, where a case of the highest importance was awaiting his presence. It was the imperative summons of the law, and the loyal advocate obeyed. Failing thus in producing the talent we have offered you upon the programme, we have nevertheless made a valuable discovery, to wit: that all the eloquence and ability of New-York does not center in the gentlemen who have disappointed us; and I have now the honor to introduce a gentleman who has not long been a resident of your city, but who is already known by reputation to every member of your community, the Rev. George H. Hepworth, who will now address you. [Applause.]

Address of Rev. GEO. H. HEPWORTH.

LADIES AND GENTLEMEN :—

It is peculiarly embarrassing to stand here in the place of the gentlemen in order to listen to whom, you have braved the inclemency of the weather. I am reminded by my position of an illustration. It is told of Oliver Wendell Holmes that he was once waited upon by a committee who desired him to fill the place of Mr. Rufus Choate on the platform of a lyceum. He stood before his audience and said : "Ladies and Gentlemen. I do not propose to *fill* Mr. Choate's place, but with your permission I will wabble around in it for hour." [Great laughter and applause.] I do not propose to fill the place of the honorable gentlemen whom you expected to hear on this platform; I cannot speak in their eloquent phrases; but the wish of my heart is just as warm

as theirs, and my word of congratulation is just as sincere.
[Applause.] Gentlemen of the Association: I do most
heartily congratulate you upon having reached your fiftieth
birthday. You look indeed well, hale and hearty. You
bear your years and your honors nobly. You have a position largely influential in this community; and you have
money that is paying a good per centage; and my great
wish is that I may be here in your midst when the one
hundredth anniversary comes around, [laughter] and when
laden down with honors, yet buoyed up with the prayers of
the tens of thousands whom you have saved, or helped to
save, you will give to the New-Yorkers of that day a report
as glowing as that which your President has given to us to-
night. I cannot speak too warmly of the value of an Institution of this kind. Every man here, who has gray hairs,
knows its value. It has been to him perhaps a rod and a
staff upon which he has been able to lean in times of doubt
and in moments of toil and perplexity.

When a boy comes from a New England or from a New-
York village into this great place, he brings with him not
only the prayers of his mother and the good advice of his
old father, but also a noble burden of boyish purity of heart.
He is buoyed up with large and golden dreams which
he hopes by hard work to crystalize into solid reality in
some day in the future. But the moment he touches your
sidewalk he feels the chill of the social atmosphere. It is
no longer *home* to him. The old roof protects him no more.
He must depend wholly upon his own resources, and he
must use alone his own energies. With only a few dimes
in his purse, and with all his worldly dry goods done up in
a bandanna pocket handkerchief he searches around among
the palaces on the avenue for a home, but every door is
shut. He goes into some by-street, hoping to live for a few
weeks on the first floor, but he cannot pay the rent. He
goes up one flight of stairs, but again the janitor shakes his

head. He goes up another flight, and again the honest
shake of the head ; and so, up and up, and up, that pure
boy goes with his bandanna pocket handkerchief until he
stands on the upper floor, and can reach up and touch the
roof. What a strange contrast between his kindly home
and that place! No sister, no mother, no friend! He is
all, all alone, in the midst of an immense populace.
He has no one who can strike palms with him. He
has no one who can give him a gentle word of advice
or of admonition. His day's work over, he sits in his
room, reading by the dim, uncertain light of his penny
dip until he is worn out and weary. Then he takes his
hat and goes out upon the side-walk. He wanders from
street to street, and curiously enough, Satan, who seems to
be ubiquitous, has opened a thousand door-ways, and he
stands in each one of them, his horns and hoofs concealed,
and beckons with gentle hand the youth to enter. Here is
a counter, and across the counter is placed the ruby wine;
and the boy is tempted. And here sits a syren singing to
him, and weaving little by little her spider web, hoping to
catch the fly, and when he is helpless to rob him of his all.
And, here and there, and everywhere these doors are open;
and yet for him there is no word of admonition—no strong,
calm, holy, beautiful friendship to which he can cling. And
so after a few months his honor becomes almost inevitably
dimmed just as the impalpable rust gathers upon the polished
surface of the steel blade when you breathe upon it. If
now in an auspicious moment he looks around and sees
some such Institution as this which you represent to-night,
and hears cheerful voices, and crosses the threshold and
sees the reading-room, with its books and magazines and
quarterlies, with its papers filed in every corner, the desire for information seizes upon him, he takes a book out of
your library, and carries it home with him ; and he reads
the next night an hour longer by his penny dip, than he did

2

the night before; and thus you, unconsciously to your-selves, have really reached out a helping hand to that man, and perhaps you have saved him from the bottomless pit of a loss of his self-respect, the pit of ruin, of present im-purity and of moral degradation. [Applause.] Who can count the value of the Institution which lifts to its mast-head such a banner as that, not only of relief, but of sal-vation? A word of advice, generously and nobly given, sometimes saves a soul; and a kind word is like a seed dropped into the ground. You may not see it to-day; it is buried out of sight by the dews of evening; but when the morning sun comes warm and fresh and drives that night away, the seed sends up its little shoot and at last comes the blossom and the fruit. Just so it is with such an Institution as this. A word here to-night, a word there in your lecture room, a book taken from the shelf here, a newspaper taken from the pile there—each one of these in-strumentalities in the hands of God's Providence may, in such a city as this, be the means of lifting up a desponding heart and of putting new energy into a despairing soul. I have but one word to say of you, God bless the work that you have done, and God grant that you may indeed mow a wide swath in the future.

The moment a boy comes to New-York, the one idea which he gets is concerning the necessity of making money. That becomes his heaven. That is what all New-Yorkers work for. The Frenchman's idea of heaven is that of a place in the midst of which there is a huge Republic with no Napoleon III; a Republic in which every citizen is a member of the Provisional Government, a Republic which maintains a standing army whose special business it is to wipe out the defeats of Metz and Strasburg. The English-man's idea of the future is immense landed estates and a title to nobility of which he forms the prominent part. But a New-Yorker's idea of heaven is a corner lot [laughter] and a free stone front; and a Government contract once a year. [Renewed laughter.]

And every single boy who comes from the country expects that corner lot, and every boy works for it for the first twenty years of his business life; and he puts into the realization of that dream all the muscle of his body, all the energy of his mind and all the strength of his soul. You, gentlemen, who are gray-headed, who are within the reach of my voice, can corroborate my words. You came to this great city years and years ago with nothing. Now you have your corner lot, and you are satisfied. And what the young gentlemen whom I represent here to-night want is a corner lot just like yours. Yet, in the attainment of such a desire, what dangers there are! The thirst for gold grows hotter and hotter. The appetite grows mightier by what it feeds upon, until at last the man becomes restless, weary, worn and tired and lies down, perhaps in defeat. But your Institution comes in when he is fresh in his manly prime. While the golden curls yet cluster around his brow, before the blue eyes have lost anything of their lustre, and while the memory of his old home on the hillside, and the dear thoughts of father and mother cling around him, your Institution comes to him and reaches out its warm, friendly, generous hand, and takes hold of his heart, and under its influences he bears those principles and those virtues out of which the only sturdy and true manhood is made. [Applause.]

I remember once, while standing upon the sea shore, to have seen a sight at once grand and awful. The waves were running mountain high, and in their madness seemed to throw their white caps to the very clouds. I looked off in the distance and saw a full rigged ship. She came rolling along from wave to wave, and I knew, but the captain did not, that there was a great rock between her and me. The man who trod the quarter-deck felt secure. He was sure of his seamanship. He thought that he was master of the situation. All at once the vessel struck the solid rock, and then all was consternation and terror on board. The waves, like a great, merciless, ruthless giant, lifted up the noble craft in its great arms and then dropped it on the rock again. In a moment a dozen men were standing by my side. They unlocked the door of a house on the beach and took out the lifeboat. In an instant those dozen men were in the boat and were pulling as if for their lives. They did not care for their own safety. There was a manly pulse in every heart, and a manly thrill in every nerve. They pulled as though each man were a father, and he was trying to save his only child. Over the waves they went and then back they came with a load of shipwrecked passengers. I looked again from the hill top and there were passengers scattered here and there in the water. The boat pulled out bravely once more, and picked up the drowning ones, here a little child in its mother's arms, and there a gray haired sire who was struggling to keep the few short hours that yet remained to him, and brought all safely to the land. And then all our hearts went up in thanksgiving to God that society had builded that house in time of peace when the ocean was calm and quiet, so that when the ocean was storm-tossed, strong men might save the helpless.

Brothers! you are doing a work like unto that. There are breakers all over your city, and many and many a young man is drawn through the maelstrom into the whirlpool, and goes down never to be seen again. Their number is not to be counted. You see them one moment, and then they are gone forever. Such an Institution as this is the expression of a desire on the part of the great community to have lifeboats all along the coast, and to man them with those who can be brave and true. And so I say to you to-night—and it is a simple word, and yet it is warm from my heart—God bless you, young men, in the grand work

which you are doing.   I give you my hand and say, God in
the Heavens give you good speed.   [Great Applause.]

The President: We have heard from the Press and from
the Pulpit, and it will be our privilege, later in the evening,
to hear from the Bar.   I now have the pleasure of introducing to you a merchant of New-York, Mr. W
Dodge.   [Applause.]

Address of WILLIAM E. DODGE, Esq.

Mr. PRESIDENT—When you called upon me, about dusk,
with such a disconsolate face, and with your programme all
broken to pieces, I could hardly resist your request to
come and say a word in behalf of the Mercantile Library
Association.   [Applause.]

It is well for us, fellow citizens, once in a while, to stop,
amid the pressing cares of business, and look around us to
see what we have in our city which is stable and likely to
last.   And it is well occasionally to look back, as time
passes rapidly, take our observation, and see where we
are going.

A very venerable clergyman, now nearly eighty, yet with
some strength and much spirit left, was called upon to see
whether—remembering the early history of the Mercantile
Library and his love for it—he would not come here to-
night and open this meeting with prayer.   After giving the
reasons why he could not come, he said: " Fifty years.!
Why, that isn't much."   [Laughter.]   No, it is not a very
great while ; but how many things have transpired since
fifty years ago ! New-York was a very small place when this
Library was organized.   It then had just about one-eighth
of its present population.   In 1820 we had only one hundred and twenty-three thousand inhabitants.   The bound-
ary of New-York was then a little beyond Canal Street ;
and those of us who were clerks in that day were away
down town ; and those of us who were in the dry goods

stores were all in Pearl Street. There was no other place for the wholesale dry goods business but Pearl Street. Then we were without Croton water, without gas, without steamboats, without railroads, without telegraphs. What were we then? What are we now? And this Mercantile Library, that has grown so great in the last fifty years, what will it be when it shall have lived a century? To-day it has an income of sixty thousand dollars a year, and a property worth half a million of dollars. You heard the President say that the Library had outgrown its present home. It will not be long before the city, in its upward flight, will leave Astor Place too far down town. Long before the next fifty years shall have rolled around, this Association, with its income of eighty or one hundred thousand dollars, will have accumulated a library such as none other will be found in this land ; and this for the instruction, the benefit, and the elevation of the coming merchants of New-York. Eleven thousand young men are now members of the Mercantile Library Association. They are *young* men, clerks, soon to take the place of the merchants of New-York, and of the land. O how much they owe already, and how much they will owe to you, as in the future they look back to the Mercantile Library ! [Applause.]

Friends, this library belongs to *us*. It is the Mercantile Library of *New-York*. Let us cherish it. Let us become better acquainted with it. Let us interest the youth more in it. Let us who are advancing in life encourage it. [Applause]. A few years ago there was a debt of sixty-five thousand dollars on the building. The young men were invited to come together, and books were distributed among them, and they went out among the merchants, and asked that this debt might be removed, and the interest which they were then paying on the mortgage might be devoted to the purchase of valuable books. The merchants responded ;

the debt was paid; and that noble building, now unencumbered, belongs to the merchants' clerks of New-York. [Applause.] We are here to-night to celebrate the fiftieth anniversary of the Library. Having looked down upon its past years, which have been so prosperous, let us look forward with hope to the fifty years that are to come. May its past prosperity be the security and the surety of what it shall be in the future. [Applause.]

The President: There is a gentleman in the hall who came here with no intention of speaking, but who has kindly consented to say a few words; and I am sure that you will thank me for introducing, as the next speaker, the Rev. Henry C. Potter. [Applause.]

Address of Rev. HENRY C. POTTER, D. D.

Mr. PRESIDENT—It was a part of the contract under which I was wrested from my seat and brought, almost forcibly, to this platform, that if the honorable Mayor of the City of New-York should appear, and say his own words in his own place, I was to be released. It was because the Mayor was supposed to be laden down with a new kind of responsibility to-night, that it was thought that perhaps he might not be here. But since I have been upon the platform, we have seen his benign countenance beaming upon us; and we have the assurance of our own eyes—as I heard a cockney Englishman express it this morning, when he opened his newspaper and read the result of yesterday's election—that "'All is well!" [Great laughter and applause.]

I cannot, however, resist the temptation which is offered me to express the feeling which was uppermost in my mind when I came here this evening; and that was the feeling of thankfulness with which I came to this meeting. I think I may claim to be, perhaps, the only one of my profession, who is here this evening, who can be said to have found his way to the ministry through the Mercantile Library. I am proud to remind myself, to-night, that I was once a merchant's clerk; and that I owe a large part of my enthusiasm for letters, if any I have, to the impetus which I received within the alcoves of the Mercantile Library. [Applause.] It was there that, as a boy, I first learned to love, not only the great literary heroes of the past, and not only the men of letters of our own day, who have been named to you to-night, but to love and revere, long before I ever saw him, the author of *Thanatopsis*. [Great applause.] Mr. Bryant has sketched for us a picture of the future, when some of the young men of another and a later generation shall take down from their shelves the well-worn books of the past, and will recall with something of curiosity, and something of admiration, the names of the men of letters who had delighted these earlier generations. May I not say, to-night, after the graceful and eloquent words which we have heard from his lips, that if there be any name then vividly remembered and cherished, it will be the name of him whom the *Westminster Review*, only the other day, called the Prince of our American Poets—William Cullen Bryant. [Great applause.]

I am pleased to be here to-night for another reason; and that is, because the very title of this institution marries two words, which it is the temptation of too many men of letters in our day to attempt to divorce. This is a *mercantile library*, an institution recognizing the value of literature, under the auspices of commerce. You have been told, very often, that New-York can never hope to be a great literary centre; that it is too much immersed in business; and the picture drawn by my brother, who has just spoken to you, of the wide-spread prevalence of an ambition for corner lots, has been supposed to apply to every man who comes to New-York and makes money. But, Mr. President, when we come to look about this great city, what are the buildings which we see standing upon so many of the finest corner lots? How many corner lots are covered by that noble institution which has contributed so largely to literature and the arts—the Cooper Institute? [Applause.] The Astor Library stands upon another corner lot; and the Lenox Library will stand upon another. [Applause.]

I desire here, as an ex-merchant, to call to mind the noble service rendered to literature by merchants, in the early and materialistic days of this Republic. The finest private library of which I have any knowledge is in the dwelling of a merchant in Cincinnati. I doubt not there are finer here in New-York; but I have not been permitted to become personally acquainted with them. Let us not, then, indulge in the fallacy that there is any hostility between a high and elevated commerce and a high and elevated literature. Let us recognize the fact, that this modern civilization of ours educates a spirit which makes them go hand and hand, and that wherever the white wings of commerce carry the freightage of our western hemisphere, there, also, will be wafted the literature that is to enlighten distant nations. [Applause.]

Many of our New England friends are fond of drawing a contrast between New England and New-York—between the spirit that reigns in and about Boston and the spirit that reigns here; yet I venture to say, that, of the young men, educated by this Mercantile Library, familiar with its literature, privileged there to commune with the society of the past and of the present, and to forget that social chill of which my brother Hepworth has spoken, in better company, perhaps, than most young men could find anywhere else in New-York—in the company of Milton and Shakespeare, of Chaucer and Spencer; and of the still greater lights of the past, of Dante, done into English by our own Longfellow; and of Homer, done into English verse by our own Bryant—[applause]—finding inspiration in such society, I venture to say that our New England friends will never be able to tell of us such a story as I heard Mr. Thos. Hughes narrate, the other day, in the company of a few friends, of a man who was born in New England, and who had spent his life not a great way from the Hub. He had gone, as a great many New Englanders are in the habit of doing, to visit the home of Longfellow, not merely because it is the abode of Longfellow, but because it was once the temporary home of Washington. Mr. Longfellow found him in the hall, and escorted him over the house, not certain whether he came to see the house on *his* account, or because of its early associations. When the stranger had gone over the house from the top to the bottom, and came again to the front door, he said, "I thank you for the privilege that you have given me, sir. It is a great thing to have seen the house where Washington ate and slept!" And then, turning to Mr. Longfellow, he said, "And what might your name be?" "My name is Longfellow," said the poet. "Longfellow?" with an air of reflection for a moment or two; "Any relation to *Abner* Longfellow, down in New Bedford?" [Great laughter and applause.]

I venture to say, Mr. President, that if the Mercantile Library continues to render the same service to the young men of New-York that it has already done, we shall not be guilty of so gross an ignorance here in this commercial and unliterary city.

I add my hearty good wishes to those that have been already expressed here to-night for the prosperity of this Society. I have the fondest personal memories of its influence, and the most abundant hopes of its glorious and enlarged future. [Great applause.]

THE PRESIDENT:—

> "Then said the mother to her son,
>   And pointed to his shield;
> 'Come with it when the battle's done,
>   Or on it—from the field.'"

Amid the perplexing difficulties that seem to have surrounded our assembling here to-night, it is an encouraging thought that notwithstanding the alarm and confusion of that fatal yesterday, we have one tried soldier with us who has done even better than by coming to us on his shield— by coming *with* it. [Applause.]

The last office that I have to perform to-night is to introduce to your kindly attention, his Honor, Mayor Hall. [Long continued applause.]

Address of Hon. A. OAKEY HALL.

I thank the Rev. Dr. Potter, of Grace Church, for his benediction. After it, I feel like a Potter's broken vessel. After Grace, should come meat; but I bring only an epilogue. One of the speakers said that he felt very much embarrassed by the absence of the gentlemen upon this programme; on the contrary *I* feel very much relieved. If one has an onyx, and not an emerald or a ruby, he does not wish to place it in a circlet of diamonds. I come therefore merely to speak the epilogue; and I remember to have heard it well said that an epilogue ought to be short, and should be crisp. I also remember that for him who pronounces the epilogue there is generally inserted on the programme, lest his vanity be wounded, this sentence: " Ladies " and gentlemen are requested to remain until the close of " the performance, as their going out disturbs the harmony " of the occasion." I am perfectly willing, however, that any one should go out; and I feel utterly lost of late, unless there is about me, as a speaker, some buzz, much confusion, and a great deal of contention. [Laughter.]

Your programme, Mr. Chairman, is certainly one on which any gentleman might feel proud to be placed; and it is certainly a programme very fitting for the name of a public man, as I perceive that your musical selection begins with " Solid Men," and has for its finale " Popular Airs."

Both are appropriate selections for this Institution. [Laughter.]

It is very appropriate that the City of New-York, in its civic authority, should be here to add the great voice of the Metropolis to the chorus sung by Mr. Hepworth: "God speed the Mercantile Library on the occasion of its Fiftieth Anniversary." [Applause.] I am happily relieved from saying anything about your Institution, because the whole ground has been already occupied; and I will therefore confine myself to epilogue. I wish, however, in reference to a remark thrown out by my friend, Dr. Potter, to remind him and you that the phrase, "Mercantile Library," is very appropriate and very memorable, because the first public library that was founded in Europe after the dark ages began to merge into the dawn of civilization, was founded by a *merchant* in the City of Florence, by the name of Nicholas Nicoli. You are here to-night to celebrate the growth of your fifty-year old library; but some time when you have the leisure, when in those pleasant alcoves yonder, in the quiet of the library, search among the volumes and trace for yourselves the wonderful growth that a few hundred years has wrought, in books and in libraries, from the time when the library of Oxford consisted of a few tracts in a chest; or from the time when the library of the Abbey of Croyland consisted of a few volumes, which could not be loaned except under penalty of excommunication—a sentence which was then considered by all classes as worse than hanging or execution for treason. That was a long time ago, several more times than fifty years. There was another library existing about that time, in which the books were chained lest they should be taken out, so valuable were they deemed. And for scores of years were books in private libraries thus chained, so that readers obtained the milk of their literature as a dairy maid returns with rich cream from the kine that have been tethered in rich pastures, lest they be injured by too much roaming for food.

As a New-York civic authority, I class all libraries, and especially this Mercantile Library, as coming under the class of the magnificent dispensaries of this city. Other dispensaries take care of the body; but over the portals of all public libraries may be written the sign words which, according to Diodorus, were written over the portals of the first Egyptian public library, and which translated reads, " *Medicine of the Mind.*"

In this luxurious age, in comparison with the prices of other things, the fee of five dollars per year almost makes this institution a *free* library; and I am happy to know that, although it is not nominally or technically free, it is, unlike a certain *free* library, open at night, so that the working man may obtain access to it. And I take this occasion briefly to announce—since reference has been made to Mr. Cooper—that it is in contemplation by the city authorities, to adopt a suggestion of his, and by his aid, and the assistance which I think the public treasury, with the assent of all parties, may give, to create an entirely free lending library in the City of New-York. [Applause.] And it may be that the Mercantile Library may be captured for that purpose, and converted into a free lending library—the city giving it full and proper indemnity for the loss of its dues. That would do no wrong to you, or to the incorporators; and would make all the people of this great city members of your Association.

I cannot finish my epilogue without indulging a pardonable pride, by stating that twenty-five years ago my humble name was inscribed upon your books; and often, amid the roar of the metropolis, I have to recollect with gratitude the cozy quietude of those dear reading-rooms in old Clinton Hall, in the very centre of a circle that now may well be described as the reading-room of the world, for, within tha circle radiates—to, at least, the American world—the news-paper literature of this country.

Fifty years ago! Why, gentlemen, it is your golden wedding! Shakespeare says, "Let us not to the marriage of true minds admit impediment." Do not libraries, in one sense, wed true minds for discussion, and for the pleasant interchanges of mental life?

Long, in the future of the City of New-York, may this Association thrive as wonderfully and deservedly as it has in the past. Long into its portals may there throng, not only merchants and clerks, but their wives and daughters, to shut out, for a brief time at least, the perplexities of business and society. And long may its subscribers, each time on entering the library, recall the beautiful salutation of the Copenhagen librarian, commencing,

"*Salvete aureoli mei libelli*,"

which may be rendered thus:

> Hail, my books! my golden treasures!
> Objects of delicious pleasures,
> Whom my eyes rejoicing please,
> Whom my hands in rapture seize;
> Introducing wits and sages,
> Lights who beamed through many ages,
> Then left to leaves their conscious story,
> And dared to trust *to you* their glory
> And their hopes of fame achieved;
> Them, dear books, you ne'er deceived!

[Applause.]

THE FIFTH

ANNUAL DINNER

OF THE

EX-OFFICERS' UNION,

AT

DELMONICO'S,

THURSDAY EVENING,

NOVEMBER 10, 1870.

Fifth Annual Dinner.

The Fifth Annual Dinner of the Officers' Union of the Mercantile Library Association, was given at Delmonico's, Thursday evening, November 10th, 1870.

Mr. H. N. CAMP presided, and on his right were Alexander T. Stewart, Esq., A. J. Mundella, M.P., Hon. Henry Hilton, Rev. Henry C. Potter, Abram S. Hewitt, Esq., Samuel Sloan, Esq., Thomas H. Faile, Esq., Edmund Coffin, Esq., Wm. E. Dodge, Jr., Esq., J. B. Vermilye, Esq., Henry Clews, Esq., Hon. Lyman Tremaine, and Isaac H. Bailey, Esq.; upon his left were Hon. Stewart L. Woodford, Hon. Wm. E. Dodge, Daniel James, Esq., Peter Cooper, Esq., Maj.-Gen. Irwin McDowell, Richard Lathers, Esq., Hon. Smith Ely, Jr., Hon. Samuel S. Cox, M.C., Maj.-Gen. Alexander S. Webb, Rev. William Adams, D.D., Rev. C. C. Tiffany, E. L. Godkin, Esq., and J. R. Kennedy, Esq.

After the dinner, the Chairman, in proposing the first toast of the evening, said:

Fellow Members of the Officers' Union: Again we are permitted to meet together around these festive boards, and to celebrate in a fitting manner this, our fifth anniversary, and the fiftieth anniversary of the Mercantile Library Association; an Association to which all of us, during some period of our lives, have given a portion of our thoughts and of our time. You will, I hope, permit me on this occasion, very briefly indeed, to congratulate you on the success which has attended our efforts in the formation and carrying

3

on of this Society. Unlike many of the societies of New-York,—the *St. Nicholas*, the *New England*, and the *St. George*—which have for their object the calling of men together of one clime, country, state or city, for charitable purposes, we are banded together for the purpose of renewing old associations, of reviving friendships that else were dead ; of re-enkindling our affections, and keeping alive our love for an Institution, which, in our earlier days, was to us a friend, a counsellor, a guide. [Applause.] And to give to the Board of Direction that may be in power, whatever aid we may in carrying on the great work of this Institution. That the object of our Society has been attained, I need only refer you to the scene before you to-night. [Applause.]

During the year nothing has occurred in our Society of marked importance. Our members are about the same in number as last year. We have had a few withdrawals, and a few admissions, so that the number has remained about the same. From the very nature of the case, drawing our membership only from a limited number as we do, (for only ex-officers can be members,) we cannot expect any large increase in any one year ; nor can we at any time expect to number many more members than we have at present. I think that I may say, however, that we have upon our rolls to-day about all the live, active, energetic members of the various boards which have preceded the present very able one. [Applause.]

It is always pardonable for those who have been connected with an institution, in its management, to look with pride and satisfaction upon the success which it has attained ; and we are very apt to think that some measure, perchance, put forward during the time that we were ourselves members, has been largely instrumental in the success of the Society. As ex-officers, we have a great and enduring pride in the success of the Mercantile Library Association, and in the position which it holds to-day among the kindred institutions of the country and of the world. When we look back to the time when we ourselves were connected with the Institution as officers; or if we go still further back, to the time when with feeble, uncertain breath, it first showed signs of life; or later, to the time when such men as Philip Hone, and John K. Leavitt, and Lawrence Nash, aided our infancy; or still later, when such men as Wilson G. Hunt, and others, came to us, and aided in placing our building out of debt—I say, when we look on that picture, and then on this, we may well feel proud, nay, honored in having been, no matter how humbly, connected with the management of an Institution that has done, and is destined to do so much good to our beloved City of New-York. [Applause.]

There are one or two features connected with our institution, which I think are worthy of especial attention. Until within a few years, since which the Clinton Hall Association has furnished volumes to our library, the whole accumulation of one hundred and twenty thousand volumes has been the result of a careful, wise, earnest husbandry of the receipts of the members for dues. With two or three exceptions, our library has never been the recipient of bequests. When you remember that out of this fund (and the dues for many years were but two dollars per year, I think for about forty years, and then three dollars, and now four,) the whole expenses of our library, with its necessarily large clerical force, have been paid, you will readily see how honestly, how well, how judiciously the affairs of our institution have been managed since its very organization. [Applause.] As I said before, our library, with two or three exceptions, has never been the recipient of any bequests. The question has often occurred to me, and I doubt not to many others—why is this? why is it that our merchants, in their large hearted liberality, dispensing their charities with a princely hand, have not remembered an institution like this? It appears to me that there is no way in

which money can do more good than by having the interest
of it provide books for the young.   I beg to commend this
thought to the moneyed men of New-York, hoping that
the seed may fall in rich ground, and bear fruit a thousand
fold. [Applause.]

The great and pressing need of to-day—and if the pressing need of to-day, how much more of the future?—is a
new, large, fire-proof building, to contain the treasures that
we already own. [Applause.] The question is, how shall
this be attained? We have called upon the good citizens
of New-York frequently, and our appeals have never been
in vain; nor do I think we shall appeal to them again in
vain. But you, the members of the Officers' Union, will
have a duty to do in this regard. Work must be done before we can obtain this desideratum to which we all look
forward with so much of interest. I am confident that the
members of our library, in expecting from the merchants
of New-York a liberal response to the call which will, I
trust, be made on them one of these days, will not be disappointed. [Applause.]

But I will detain you no longer. We have with us to-
night very many distinguished gentlemen, from many of
whom we expect to hear. I shall therefore close the few
remarks I have made by offering the first regular toast of
the evening :

" The State of New-York, an empire based on the will of
the people. While the foundation lasts, the superstructure
is imperishable."

The Governor of the State was expected to be here to
speak to this toast. He was called to Albany ; but we have
Ex-Lieutenant-Governor Woodford here. [Cheers.] In
writing his acceptance of our invitation, he says: "It will
give me great pleasure to be with you, provided Governor
Hoffman has not sent me so far up Salt River that I cannot
get back in time." [Great laughter and applause.] The

fact that he is with us is evidence enough that he has not been sent so very far in that direction; and is further evidence that he is ready and willing to stand half a dozen such defeats as he has had within the last three days. [Cheers and applause.]

Hon. STEWART L. WOODFORD.

Mr. Chairman and Gentlemen of the Mercantile Library Association,—There may be a possible fitness in my speaking to you in response to the "State of New-York;" for within the last seven weeks I have *visited* most of the State [applause], and have found safe return to my New-York home by the way of Salt River. [Renewed laughter and applause.] Our *State* should touch our love and our pride very deeply. We are in the centre of the Atlantic chain. To this point the wealth and the enterprise of our merchants brings whatever this entire nation needs for its use, from the lands beyond the sea. Here the cotton and the sugar of the South, the corn and the wheat of the North-West, the ore of Pennsylvania, the manufactures of New England and of the Middle States, find their market and their sale. To you, as mercantile men, I need say nothing, either of what New-York has done in the past, of what she is in the present, or of what she so justly promises to be in the future. We occupy a position, both geographically, and because of our wealth and power, that imposes large responsibilities upon all New-Yorkers. We should be radical in striving to secure all that may add to the wealth, to the culture, and to the highest prosperity either of our State or of the Union. [Applause.] We should be conservative in holding all that is good in the past, that it may be the seed corn of our growth in the years to come. And more than that—and now I speak to you as young men—you should do your duty, not merely as merchants— the plethoric pocket-books that rustle with greenbacks under each table indicate that you have done that already [a laugh]—but if we would have our State and nation be what she should be, the young men of the land should not forget themselves in the mere scrambling for the dollars. [Applause.] You should cling to all that is best in culture, to all that is broadest in education, to all that is highest and most beautiful in art. You should make your Mercantile Library, with its magnificent accumulation of books, its courses of scientific lectures, its work in the preparation of young men—you should make it the flower that typifies the beauty of your commercial endeavor, as the wealth of your merchants typifies and illustrates its success. [Great applause.] While toiling in the counting-room, the storehouse, or the bank, do not forget that your brains are worth more than your pockets—that an idea in your head that shall be a power to you and a life to your fellows, is worth more than a thousand added to your bank account. Do not forget another thing: that you, young men, to whatever party you may belong, should give your best thought, your most earnest endeavor, to make the politics of your State and of your land pure, honest, efficient for the real up building of the people; for, for the up-building of the peoples all democracies and all republics were instituted and made. [Applause.] Your toast has said that so long as New-York rests upon the will of the people, the superstructure will be enduring. See that your young men are educated. See that your young men are honest. See that they stand by that which is best, which is purest, which is most progressive—alike in business and in politics. [Applause.] Remember another thing: that when the strife and the bitterness of these annually recurring elections are past, that our State and nation rises as something better than party, something higher than platform, something to which all good citizens should give their most loving prayers, and their most earnest effort. [Applause.] See to it, that in the public life of all your officials, you are ready to approve that which is right, whether the officer be with you in political theory or opposed to you; see to it that you are ready to condemn that which is wrong, whether the actor be with you in sentiment or be opposed to you. [Great applause.]

Let us all, one and all, without regard to the lines that have divided us, and that shall divide us in political struggles, do our whole duty as New-Yorkers, as citizens, and as earnest, true-hearted young men. [Applause.]

Allow me, in closing, to propose a volunteer toast:

"The Governor of the State of New-York: may he be supported in all that is right, and generously and fairly criticised in all that is wrong." [Applause.]

THE CHAIRMAN: I give you as the second regular toast:

"The City of New-York: unequaled in the splendor of her geographical position, she welcomes, through her eastern portal the citizens of the Old World, and from her western gates issue myriads of people of the New. Long the chief city of America, soon to become the metropolis of the world."

Until about six o'clock, his Honor, Mayor Hall, was expected to be present and respond to this toast, as he promised to do, and as we know he desired to do. But at half-past six he writes us: "The cold, raw wind has shut up my vocal organs, already heavily taxed." So we cannot have a response from the Mayor of our City. But among our guests we have one who talks well upon any subject I ever heard him talk upon; and I shall take the liberty of calling upon him to respond to this toast—the Hon. S. S. Cox, sometimes called "Sun-Set Cox;" but day before yesterday he proved that there was no *sun-set* to his name. [Applause.]

Hon. S. S. COX.

Gentlemen: I came here this evening fully prepared to respond to a toast of a different order—thoroughly accomplished, as I supposed, to speak on quite another theme. I was put down at the end of the roll, on the old toast to "Woman;" and I reckoned that, by the end of the feast, we might all become so oblivious to eloquence, that my duty could be easily discharged. But I am called to a different task, and to one which should have been discharged by our worthy Mayor. I suppose the Mayor is at home, and if not looking after his famous figures of speech, he is doubtless ciphering up the figures of the late election. [Laughter.] I feel very incompetent to respond to the toast which has been so kindly proposed by my friend, the chairman. I feel my inability to speak in this volunteer manner, not only my inability, mentally, to speak for the big City of New-York, but I feel very disproportionate physically, for any such effort. You must therefore excuse me from making anything but a very short speech.

The dominant idea of your toast is, that New-York sits here as the gateway of the nations, as the great thoroughfare through which, not only commerce and trade, but the very people are moving, as if by some divine order, to the great West. As I come from the land of *sunset*, a land powerful in arms, as my old comrade, Gen. McDowell, can illustrate, and rich in her beautiful soil, as all your granaries and elevators demonstrate, I can speak, in one sense, for that great West; and as your toast connects the West with the East, and New-York with the outland and the inland, I would for a moment make a little horoscope for your city.

New-York has just begun her great career. She will be the metropolis, not only of this hemisphere, but of this globe. She is destined to be so. [Applause.] The island of Manhattan was never intended as a mere pasturage. It was never intended, as the first Dutchmen tried it, merely for raising cabbages, or grass. You cannot sub-soil New-York so well as you can some other parts of our great country. New-York was intended, not for agriculture, not for farming, nor yet for forest; but it was set as a great jewel on the very brow of the ocean, that all nations might send to her their people and their commerce. She reaches out her hand to all the world, or would reach it, if her better day in commerce were dawning, which I sincerely hope. [Applause.] If New-York continues to increase in the future as she has in the past forty years, I think it is no exaggeration to say that New-York, at the end of a century, will have six millions of people; and that the nation, of which New-York will be the metropolis, will then have a hundred millions. I do not mean to say that the island of Manhattan will alone have six millions of people; but we shall do what other cities have done, we shall push over to Brooklyn and Williamsburg, and draw that distant Jersey —[a laugh]—somewhat nearer to New-York, and make one grand metropolis of all. [Applause.] Young men here, to-night, will live to see New-York City a city of six millions; and I believe that some of our elder men here will also live to see it. I will conclude my response by wishing you all a life so long that you may see New-York City with a population of six millions, and attend the Centennial Anniversary of the Mercantile Library Association. [Laughter and applause.]

The Chairman—The next toast is the one which is the nearest to our hearts:

"The Mercantile Library Association; a half century of steadily increasing usefulness constitutes its appropriate eulogy."

Of course, there is but one person in the room who can appropriately respond to a toast like this, the very able and energetic President of the Association, Mr. M. C. D. Borden.

M. C. D. BORDEN, Esq.

Mr. President and Gentlemen :—One of our later novelists in one of his most pleasing efforts, for the moment abandons his fiction to give place to a most truthful remark— "when we write a story or sing a poem of the great Nineteenth Century, I give you my sacred word of honor there is but one fear—*not* that our theme will be beneath us, but we miles below it."

So, Sir, when I undertake to speak to the Toast you have given me, I am impressed by the immensity of the subject and my utter helplessness to meet, at all adequately, its claims.

A famous writer of our own times makes Coleridge responsible for saying that if he were a clergyman in Cornwall, he should preach fifty-two sermons a year against wreckers. Having at heart the best interests of the Association which I now represent, the same spirit must be my apology for addressing you on the real poverty of our Library and its one essential want.

Mr. President, I have but one story to tell. It is that of a great Institution, conceived in the interests of that vastly numerous class to which most of us now belong—born in the obscurity of a modest enterprise—nurtured in the high purpose of its beneficent aim—filling each new year of life with a year's record of accomplished good—established at last, beyond all contingency and doubt, upon the firm basis of experiment proven a success. It is the story of an Institution that has a broad philanthropy for its object— indiscriminate good to all as its practiced motto—and a half century of faithful service, the unimpeachable evidence of a stable and permanent worth. It is the story of sunshine and storm—of conquest and defeat—of sufferance and reward; the rainbow experience that discovers through and beyond the blinding shower a pledge of bright and glowing promise. [Applause.]

It is the story of an Institution that has fought its way through weary years of cold and discouraging doubt—whetting its determination against rough difficulties and resisting force—never so near a great danger as to-day, when, with the mute appeal of its fifty well-spent years, it rests calmly and quietly in its worn-out shell to see a kindred organization celebrate its early anniversary in a stately and palatial home.* Under circumstances ordinarily incident to our festive gathering, I might content myself with a simple acknowledgement of the compliment you have offered me, pausing only to give expression to the customary sentiment of the occasion, and, in charity, find my seat in the briefest possible time.

But we are assembled under circumstances *most extraordinary*. We are about to close the book and seal the record of our semi-centennial life. What a history that volume contains! Were it my province to unfold it now, reading but a single page at random here and there, how would your hearts thrill with conscious joy and thankfulness at that long record of accomplished good!—a history of achievement and success, buoyant and full of cheer, punctuated, in the ordinary course of events, by some mistakes and many doubtful measures, but these serving only, like the mariners' trusted lights, to mark the shoals and dangers of our experience, recording now and then defeats, but writing always after them, in quick succession, the substantial evidence of greater victories—a bright chronicle, take it all in all, of usefulness and good. [Applause.] To dwell at length on this were a pleasing and a grateful task. But another book is to be written. The second part of our work begins here and to-night; and I have surely mistaken the courage and zeal, the loyalty and faith, the interest and

* The Young Men's Christian Association.

metal of past and present friends, if the first page is to be unworthy of the volume we have already closed. [Applause.]

I call your attention, then, to one fact—a fact that has been staring us in the face most suggestively for years, creeping upon us with our growth, the natural consequence of our prosperity, making itself more and more patent with expanding age, confronting us to-day with an earnestness that compels our respect and a demand that will not be ignored. It is the want, grown into the necessity, of a new, a more commodious, and a *safer* building. [Applause.]

Few enterprises exhibit the progress of our own. Not many institutions need so little, after all, to insure a perfect and lasting success. You know how modest our beginning was. You have witnessed the rapidity of our growth. You recognize in our Library of to-day a great and distinctive power for good. It is a prophecy almost fulfilled, that it is to be the greatest, the grandest, the most useful of its kind. Thus far no stain of weak indifference or thoughtless inefficiency mars its fair name. Thus far, it has kept pace with the times and the progress of our matchless city. We have seen it in Fulton Street, a half century since, the pioneer—the first of the many that have grown around it—as a distributor of books, then with a handful of volumes and a miniature hall for its less than two hundred members. Five years elapse, and we find it in another home with a multiplied list of books, a larger roll of members and a few exceptional friends among the outside world. Less than five years more, and it has moved again, this time to a building of its own—the Clinton Hall of forty years ago. A score years more are passed and the greatest and the grandest move of all, AS YET, to the Clinton Hall of to-day—its hundred members multiplied a hundred times, and a hundred volumes where it had but one.

Here then, it rests to-day, inherently strong and prosperous, abounding in books, the repository of vast and accumulative wealth in literature and art, the occupant of a building once well adapted, but already inadequate to its use—a home venerable with age, but correspondingly tottering and weak, so far from fire-proof as to be uncommonly susceptible to fire, possible of destruction, with all it contains, in a single day.   Well may we pause in the flush of a pardonable pride, to contemplate a danger so appalling ! Well may we start from our lethargy and sleep, to think and plan and ACT for our defense.   [Applause.]

First and above all, sir, I speak for the safety of our property and books.   It is the provident thought of a wise man, who discovers himself in possession of that which he values, to find some safe and secure depository for its keeping.   It is the instinct of the child.   It is the principle that underlies all others in maturer life.   The same rule of caution, inborn in our nature and a part of our very being, follows us from the cradle to youth, from youth to manhood, from manhood to the grave.   Out of this comes safety to person, security to property and home.   It is in obedience to this law of caution—everywhere recognized and obeyed—that countless wealth appears in the form of stores and storehouses, proof alike against fire and the burglar's hand.   Property is at a risk; no sacrifice is too costly to protect it.   Material possessions are threatened; how sublime the effort, how prodigal the exposure, the best of us will make in their defence.   Tell me now, where is the merchandize to match in value our ripe and well-earned harvest of books?   What fabric of the hand that hand can make again to compare in worth to the work of minds, the heritage direct from God?   Why hesitate to deal with facts?   In that building, while I speak, there are more than a hundred thousand books.   Many, aye, MOST of them, money can replace.   But out of that collection, there are a many more—rare relics of master minds, rich trophies of classic day, of which no attainable duplicates exist. There, too, lie files of the press, complete and in accessible form— the current news of to-day and days long since gone by— the world's history in detail—the authentic record of the little and the great events of life for the fifty years that have gone. Not the collection of a single year; not the result of a single lifetime. Some who have added to its aggregate have not lived to witness the growth to which the Library has attained. Many who are here will never appreciate or know the weary hours and years of toil and patient endeavor that have won for us the abundant recompense of our present power and influence.

Do I exaggerate the value of our Library? Language is *powerless* to express it. Silver and gold do *not* represent it? Do you question its usefulness? I give you back an answer from the ten thousand members who attest its worth and the hundreds who every day draw from its varied fund. Will you dare to contemplate its loss? Then you anticipate disaster which, like

> " A malady
> Preys on the heart that medicine cannot reach,
> Invincible and cureless."

No man of us all but shrinks from the simple idea of calamity like this. Away, then, with the fact which makes it possible. [Applause.] You, who come together here, as the years roll on, to eat and drink to the prosperity of your fair enterprise, have done yeoman's service in a fruitful cause. You think no labor irksome, no effort too costly, no attention close enough in the struggle for a higher and a better name. You watch—how untiringly!—the Institution's growth! You do all that man can do to accelerate and further it. You do NOT take the first and now most important step to make safe and secure the acquisition you already have. Ah! sir, it is the PREVENTIVE that we want now, and it is always cheaper than the CURE.

You tell me, perhaps, that this is no new theme, and you remind me that there has been talk enough and without result on just this very thing. Sir! there never HAS been talk enough—there never WILL be talk enough, so long as a hundred thousand books lie defenceless and exposed to fire; and you and I, and the multitude of friends the Library has, are false to our trust and false to ourselves so long as the great danger remains, while safety, absolute and complete, is within our power. The Library has no selfish end. It lives in the interest and for the good of those who accept its proffered gifts. It was made for society. Its whole purpose is for society's well-being and better estate. Let society do this much for the Library, that it shall protect and make safe its books.

Believe me, sir, this is no idle claim. It is the earnest appeal of a grand enterprise in extremity. Establish safety, and you secure success. Tolerate unnecessary danger, and you tamper with deplorable failure. Webster once said, at Rochester, "If I thought there was a stain on the remotest hem of the garment of my country I would devote my utmost labor to wipe it off." Let us take heed, gentlemen guardians of the Library, that no spot of deliberate inactivity destroy for ever the whiteness of our official robes. There stands the creature of your making. Full fifty years to-night its race has run.

> Fairer than sculptured stone,
> Nobler than lofty monuments or gilded dome,
> Proud epitaph of years to come,
> Your contribution to your race.

One thing only is undone, and the hour is ripe for its accomplishment. We have won a jewel, bright and resplendent, as the price of a half century's work. Let us hasten to find a casket WORTHY of its keeping. [Applause.]

In the light of what SHOULD be, I seem to see the old supplanted by the new—all fears and doubts dispelled—all apprehension set at rest, and our fond hopes realized to the full in the security of a grander edifice that shall save and perpetuate our mother Institution.

In the terrible siege in India, it is related that a Scotch girl raised her head from the pallet of the hospital, and spoke words of courage to the English hearts around her. " I hear the bag-pipes—the Campbells are coming." And they said, "Jessie, it is delirium." "No, I KNOW it. I heard it afar off." And after a little the pibroch rang upon their ears, and the banner of England floated triumphantly over their heads.

Even so on this, our fiftieth birth-day eve, I hear the rejoicing of a brighter day, when the crowning act of our devotion shall be JUSTICE to the Library we have made. [Long continued applause.]

The CHAIRMAN—" The Merchants of New-York—the fame of whose intelligence, energy and honor, is only outshone by the munificence of their benefactions."

It is not always at a dinner that a toast is given that contains so much of truth as the one which I have just read; and it is still more rare that the presiding officer has the privilege of calling upon one whose whole life and career has been in accordance with the sentiment of this toast, to respond, as has been the case of the gentleman upon my left, the Hon. William E. Dodge. [Applause.]

HON. WILLIAM E. DODGE.

MR. PRESIDENT AND GENTLEMEN,—We often hear of the "princely merchants of New-York." We have with us, to-night, the *Prince* of New-York Merchants.*—[applause]— and I came here, to-night, expecting to listen to a response

* Mr. A. T. Stewart.

to this toast from this prince of merchants; and it was but a moment ago that I learned that I was expected to respond. I have been thinking, while sitting here, and running my mind back over the fifty years that have passed in the history of the Mercantile Library, of the honored names of those who were the merchants of New-York when this Library Association was formed. It is well for us occasionally to stop and think of the past, and to recall the honored names of those who have long gone to their rest, and left such a heritage to us. New-York, fifty years ago, boasted of many men of noble stature. My mind has been running along through South Street, Front Street, Pearl Street and Broadway. I have thought of the Griswolds, the Howes, the Goodyears; and running along through Pearl Street, I have thought of those honored men who were the jobbing merchants when this Association was formed—the Parishes and the Palmers; and then along Broadway, of the retail merchants—Vanderbilt, the Haights, Jotham Smith and Doremus: and among the hardware men the Roosevelts, the Vanderbilts and the Kingsleys. They have all passed away, and hundreds and hundreds of their associates with them—noble men they were—and have given place to others; and the city has been passing on; and those who were the first members of this Association— where are they now? How few still linger who were with you in Fulton and in Cliff Streets! And how soon will they who now occupy the places of the merchants of New-York—the high and prominent positions—how soon will they pass away, and give place to the present members of your Association. And when fifty years more shall have passed away, and some one shall speak, as I now do of the merchants of New-York, they will run back to the present period, and speak of those who are now active; but what changes will then have taken place? What is New-York now? What was New-York then? What will New-York

4

be when another half century shall have rolled around?
How different its business is now from what it was when
your Association was formed. I was then a boy in a store
in Pearl Street. How different was business then from what
it is now. We had then our periodical seasons of business,
the Fall and the Spring. Our Winters and Summers were
as nothing. When the cold chills of November came,
it was predicted that soon the canal would close; and then
down went half of the curtains. And after a little the
North River would close, and then down went the curtains
for the rest of the Winter. [Laughter.] What would
New-York be to-day without railroads, without steamboats,
without telegraphs? We have been passing through such
wonderful changes during the last half century, that we
hardly realize what they are. What was our vast country
when this Mercantile Library was established? Chicago
had never been heard of. With the exception of St. Louis,
the entire West, now teeming with its millions of inhabitants, and interlaced with its thousands of miles of railroads, was the hunting-ground of the Indians. The ele-
ments that have been at work during the past fifty years,
making New-York what it is, and our country what it is,
will accumulate and act with increased impetus during the
fifty years to come; and no man can conceive of what New-
York City will be, or of what these United States will be,
when another fifty years shall have rolled around. [Ap-
plause.] Let the young men of New-York realize their
position and their high responsibility; and let them pre
pare themselves, by the opportunities for self-improvement
that are open to them, for the vast responsibilities that will
rest upon them when we, who now fill the places of the merchants of New-York, shall have passed away. [Applause.]

THE CHAIRMAN: "The Army and the Navy: our pride
and boast; ever ready to uphold our liberties when assailed
by foes within our borders or beyond our shores."

We have with us to-night one who, in all the positions
which he has held, has shown himself to be a man, a Christian, and a gentleman; and I shall call upon him to respond
to this toast—Major-General McDowell, of the U. S. Army.

MAJOR-GENERAL IRWIN McDOWELL.

Mr. PRESIDENT AND GENTLEMEN—If there be worlds
besides our own—and I hope there are—where there are
beings not unlike ourselves, who not only profess to be and
call themselves, but who really are Christians, and who
live a life of higher intellectuality than we do; and if
such an one were to visit us, and go abroad among the
nations of the earth (I do not mean among the savage
nations of the earth, but among the highest Christian
people), nothing, I fancy, would so utterly bewilder him as
to see the immense preparations made by all those nations
for war. Every resource of chemistry, every manufacture
of whatever description, throughout the globe—for war
always flourishes at the expense of all other trades—are
compelled to pay tribute to this end. Children are taken
at an early age, sent to school, and educated to the highest
point for that particular business. Vast numbers of men
are drawn from the ordinary, and what we would naturally
think, the proper avocations of life, and kept apart and in
training, ready for the terrible work of war. Why must
this be? Where is the necessity for such immense preparations for the destruction of our fellow-men? This is a question upon which we may speculate to almost any extent. I
only know, in my own experience, that when I first entered
the army, the great question then seemed to be settled, and
that wars were never again to take place. It was then
proposed to abolish our military organization, disband the
army, and lay up the navy, for it was thought that the era
of good feeling and peace throughout the world had been
reached. [Laughter.] Then we had the Mexican war—a war

without any necessity—a wrong done to a weak republic
and our neighbor—which commenced with a lie: "Whereas,
American blood has been shed upon American soil," which
was untrue; "And whereas, war exists by the acts of
Mexico," which was untrue; "Therefore," &c. And so we
had that war; and other wars followed. I do not speak of
the Indian wars, which were brutal acts and without any
necessity whatever. [Applause.] I have frequently found
myself in the position of warring on the weak, with the
strong, or on the side of the wrong against the right.
Why is this? Other persons than myself had better answer
that. The fact probably is, that wars always will exist in
this country where they ought never to exist, and in other
countries that profess to be far advanced in civilization.
And they break out at times and places least expected.
You all recollect how unexpected our last war was; but
it was not more so, probably, than the next will be. It
seems therefore to me, that it is our duty to see to it that
we are not wholly unprepared when the next war shall
come upon us. I have somewhere read the sentiment,
"Woe to the nation that is unfitted for war." A nation
may have arsenals and armies and vast magazines, yet all
these will avail nothing if the military spirit be wanting,
for the wolf never counteth how many sheep there be.
[Applause.]

The CHAIRMAN: "The Press of the City of New-York:
unsurpassed in intelligence, and unexcelled in enterprise
throughout the world. It has proved the Tribune of a free
people, and the active Herald of the Times. May it long pre-
serve to us the Nation, and never yield to other agencies its
Post."

We have with us to-night a gentleman who, perhaps, is
personally known to but few of us, but known to all of us
by his works; and I have great confidence that he will respond to this toast quite as ably as he edits *The Nation*.

Mr. E. L. GODKIN.

I was very much, and not altogether agreeably surprised, when I was informed that I should be expected to respond to the toast just given. I feel that I can only very inadequately and very incompletely speak for the press of New-York. The branch of it with which I am more particularly connected can hardly be said to fulfill the qualifications which constitute the strongest claim of the New-York Press to distinction—amongst which I may mention, as, perhaps, the principal, the extraordinary skill and enterprise which it shows in the collection of news. The weekly press, of course, profits by that ; but then it cannot claim credit for it; and it really looks upon the process of collecting with very much the same simple wonder as the rest of mankind does. The events of the last summer, during the European war, have, perhaps, brought home to us more vividly than ever before, the full nature and extent of the service which the daily press renders to the public in that particular field of its duty. I think it may be said also, that nobody who is unfamiliar with the machinery of the press, can really have an adequate idea of the amount of skill and ingenuity, courage, patience and energy, that is put into the "make up" of the summary of the world's news which is laid on our tables every morning. To be sure, there is some of it to which, perhaps, we are not fully entitled. We, perhaps, have a right to know all that Bismarck knows, or that Gambetta knows, or Moltke knows, of the events of the war; but we hardly have a right to full and true and particular details of battles and skirmishes of which no report has, or ever will reach the Prussian or the French headquarters ; and we have occasionally, during the summer, been treated to some such items of news. [Laughter and applause.]

The New-York Press undertakes to do a great deal —

more, I think, than the press of any other country or city; and the greater part of it it certainly does admirably well. [Applause.] It incurs, however, the penalty which usually attaches to great enterprises and the assuming of great responsibilities—in laying itself open to a great deal of fault finding. Notwithstanding the fault finding, it may be truthfully said, that if the members of all the other professions would, in proportion to their opportunities and abilities, do as much for the purification of society as the members of the press do, society would certainly before now have been rid of many and the greatest of its evils. In judging the press, we have to remember that an editor can never speak in a whisper. Whatever he has to say, he has to say through a speaking trumpet, and at the top of his voice. If, for instance, as sometimes happens, he has to express his dissatisfaction at the conduct of a brother editor, he cannot whisper it about in coteries, as the lawyer or the doctor can, but he has to proclaim it from the housetop; and this has not a tendency to raise the press in the popular steem.

The power of the press is now enormous, and the exercise of it is practically unrestrained, either by law, or by public opinion. And I think, when we consider this, and consider what human nature is, that the wonder is that this power should have been so little abused, and has, on the whole, been exercised so much for good.

I saw, the other day, in a paper for whose opinions I have great respect—the *Christian Union*—an enumeration of the wants of the day, and there was set down as one of the most serious and pressing of them all, the want of Christian editors. It occurred to me that there was one want which was still more pressing,—the want of Christian *readers*. (Applause). I think that what the economists call an effectual demand for Christian editors would be answered as readily as a similar demand for any other commodity; and the only people who can create such a demand, are Christian readers. This is simply another way of saying that the press is exactly what the community calls for. It can never be anything else. And in the new civilization, upon the first stage of which we now find ourselves, the press will undoubtedly do the greater part of the work in giving tone to society. The assertion may seem paradoxical, but the press will take its character and tone from society. The one reacts on the other. When we meet with a paper *which violates decency, which obstructs justice, or shields corruption, or drags family secrets to light,* it will not do to cast all the odium of it on the man who makes an unclean living by it. Those who read it are certainly partners, to a very great extent, in his guilt. [Applause].

There is one other point connected with the press which is pertinent in an address to an assembly like this, which is composed of gentlemen who are united by their interest in a great public library,—it is the charge which is so frequently brought against ne wpapers of being the enemies of books. One hears it constantly said that the excessive growth of newspaper reading has a tendency to drive from the world the careful thinkers, and the close students, and the patient investigators, by destroying in the public mind all taste for, and all sympathy with the results of their labors. Now, I think that if we look back during fifty years, inside of which the newspaper press may be said to have taken its rise, we shall not find much to support that charge, but on the contrary, much to upset it. Although it is true that in some branches of the arts, other ages have been much more thorough and pains-taking than our age is, nevertheless, in the fields of science and literature, which require study, and search, and patient investigation, there has been no age so thorough as ours; and, although I do not mean to say that the growth of books and the growth of the newspaper press stand to each other in the relation of cause and effect, yet I think that I am quite warranted in the assertion that the newspaper is not the enemy of books and that newspaper reading, instead of being a hindrance, is really a help to thorough investigation, patient search and severe study. The newspaper press not only multiplies readers, but it certainly does something towards providing the authors of good books. [Applause].

THE CHAIRMAN.—"The College of the City of New-York: As the Free Academy, she educated many of our noblest sons. May her usefulness increase in equal proportion to the dignity of her name."

We have with us a gentleman who is best known to us for his efforts, and for his successes upon the tented field,—ever ready to perform all the duties which he was there called upon to perform, manfully and earnestly. Of late he has been called to the Presidency of the College of the City of New-York; and I have no doubt he will fill that position with the same honor, the same integrity, and the same directness of purpose with which he fulfilled the duties of his old profession. I beg to introduce to you Major General Webb.

MAJOR-GENERAL ALEXANDER S. WEBB.

Mr. PRESIDENT and GENTLEMEN: In the first place, I must thank you for the wording of your toast. And next, I thank you for having preceded me with such earnest men as Governor Woodford, and your president, who has in such well rounded sentences, expressed so much that gives me cheer in the cause I represent.

You speak, first, of the Free Academy, and of its graduates, and you speak of them in the most flattering terms, as noble men. I come here to-night nearer to you because I have been so short a time with that institution. I can, for that reason, speak to you of it almost as one cf you, and as an outsider, but as one who has had time and opportunity to thoroughly appreciate what I doubt has ever been brought before you in proper language.   I can speak to you of its graduates,—for their records I have examined.   I can point westward, to the man who took the place of Mitchel in the observatory.   I can point to the seat of the judge.   I can point you to lawyers to the number of eighty or ninety; to the clergy—ten or fifteen; to your architects—five or six, who are now known by their names, but who are not known to you as they should be,—as the graduates of that place.   The institution has not received its credit for them ; because I assure you I do not think the earnest voice of some who have felt its influence has ever been raised in properly bringing the Institution before the thinking minds of our community.   I am here as the President of that Institution.   I am *in* the Institution, though still an army officer, and still a representative of the men who are also represented here to-night by Major-General McDowell; I am the representative of these men to do a simple duty, and to use my best endeavors, the gift of the United States Government to me.   [Applause.]

As a Free Academy, the Institution was founded for a purpose which has never, perhaps, been fully explained to those who, as citizens, cannot generally find the time to bestow upon our educational system the thought which we, who are most interested in it, feel that at many times we have a right to demand for it.   It had a double object.   It was not simply to give a higher education to those who had no money wherewith to buy it, but its object also, was to give an incentive to no less than sixty thousand youths, and to place there a high standard of education.   It has fulfilled its mission in that respect.   I say this after a careful examination—that it has raised the standard of education.   And it has done this entirely outside, and independent of all physical machinery.   The very best evidence of this that could be given, I give you in my own person, in my own election to the position I now hold.   It is there-

fore to me a sacred trust—more sacred than you could pos-
sibly believe. When I see before me each morning eight
hundred representatives of more than sixty thousand boys,
who are there, not only to receive an education, but also to
receive that which comes from that education—that manliness and independence, that feeling that if you do right you
will be carried on in the right—I feel then, and in such
times, what my responsibility is.

I have been there but one year and two short months. I
came there under the promise that it should be made what
its founders intended it should be. It is *sui generis.* You
have no right without an examination, to test it by any
other college in the land. It stands by itself. It has a
special mission. And that mission I feel that it must and
will fulfil. [Applause.] Within the City of New-York,
you have six thousand half educated boys who have been
forced to leave that institution by the want of means on the
part of their parents to support them. For the half education given those, it has seldom, if ever, received any credit
whatever. But once within its walls, once brought in con-
tact with those who will teach them that be they rich or
poor, it is the battle of the brain, it is manliness, it is integrity, it is the desire to do right, that will make the man
—once brought within its influence, I believe they are sent
out to you to be better and purer men. [Applause.]

You have here nearly six hundred graduates. I can give
you the members and show you their several callings. You
have now a Board of Education which has determined that
this college shall furnish those who shall be prepared to
teach, in a proper way, those who enter our public schools;
and I ask you, as thinking men, is it a little, is it a small
thing that we turn out five in a year who are competent to
teach, not only with the head, but with the heart? Is it a
small thing that you are thus enabled to place within our
educational system five or ten young men per year, who are

taught to believe that in educating men there is a heart, and a soul, and a fitness to the end that must go with it? That has been done within the last year; and they are now erecting upon the college grounds a school costing the miserable sum of thirty thousand dollars, which is only begged from the funds, in order that the quality of those young men may there be tested to see if they are fit to be sent out as educators of the young. I assure you that a hundred thousand a year would help you as much in that respect, as in any way that you could spend it.

I am glad that I have had the opportunity to express to you the hopes and wishes which I cherish for the Institution with which I have been for a short time connected. [Applause.]

THE CHAIRMAN.—"The Clergy of New-York—distinguished pre eminently for commending Christ's truth to the common people, and embodying his spirit of humanity in works of wide-spread beneficence."

Last night, at the Academy of Music, you were aware of the many excuses that were received by the president of the Association from the speakers that were expected to be present, and that in the stress we laid violent hands upon a gentleman whom we had invited merely as one of the hearers. He made, I doubt not you will all agree with me, one of the most telling speeches of the evening. We have laid hands upon him again, and shall ask him to respond to the toast which has been given—the Rev. Henry C. Potter, of Grace Church. [Applause.]

REV. H. C. POTTER.

MR. PRESIDENT—I was very much at home last night in taking the unprepared service that I did, because of my past relations to the merchants' clerks of this and other cities. I am not so much at home to-night in speaking for the clergy of New-York. [Laughter.] I am but a junior among the juniors; and when I am confronted at the opposite end of the table with the distinguished divine who represents the Madison Avenue Presbyterian Church, [applause,] I may well cast about for some such remote excuse for action, as I heard an Irishman relate the other day, of a friend, who chanced to meet the great poet to whom I alluded last evening, and said to him.: "Mr. Longfellow, might I shake your hand, sir?" and in excuse for the liberty, as he regarded it, he added: "Sir, I have got a brother that is a *pote*—and a drunkard, too!"   [Laughter.]

It is only as one of the most insignificant of this great brotherhood, and the youngest of them all, that I undertake at all to respond to your toast to-night. And yet if any words ought to bring a clergyman to his feet, they are the very kindly words in which you have spoken of that vocation here to-night; and surely, in the face of them, the clergy ought gratefully to remember, and I as one of them do gratefully remember, and bear testimony to the large-hearted and generous co-operation in every work of fellowship which the clergy have had from the truly princely class whom you represent. What would be the philanthropies of New-York without the purses of the merchants of New-York? It is to me one of the most cheering facts connected with the ministry in New-York, as I may speak from my short experience of it here, that wherever there is a good cause, a cause that has a bottom to it, and that is doing a direct and practical work, there is no material difficulty in getting the money to sustain it. [Applause.] Sometimes, it is true, our merchants are impatient of the constant interruptions of this sort that meet them at their business; and sometimes, as I heard the other day, they receive those interruptions somewhat irreverently, if not profanely; but, as the incident I am about to relate will show, even that irreverence generally finds its end in their habitual generosity. I was told the other day of a somewhat persistent, and not very discreet clergyman from the West, who, full of the college which he represented, went down into Wall Street and pushed his way into a banking house, and, without invitation, into the back counting-room, and, without a word of preface, stuck under the eyes of an engrossed banker there his subscription book, with the simple question: "Sir, what will you give to ——— College?" It was not very surprising (though it was certainly not very reverent), that he answered as he did—"Sir, I will give exactly one ———." I leave you to fill in the word. [Laughter.] The clergyman was a methodical man; he took his book to the corner of the room and wrote Mr. John ———, one d———." [Great laughter.] He went down the street and took his book into another counting-room; and you can imagine the sort of enthusiasm which that sort of a subscription called out there. Persons who saw it, said: "Sir, I will give you twenty-five dollars for that joke, it is worth it." [Laughter.] He went to another place and got a still better subscription. [Renewed laughter.] The story travelled down the street, as stories *do* travel down Wall Street—and presently it came back to the spot where it had originated, and the merchant who had made the impatient and profane answer, found it was going up and down Wall Street with very productive results. He followed this astute and clever parson from the West, and said to him: "Sir, this is a very good joke of yours, but it has gone quite far enough, and I want to ask you what you mean by putting my name on your book in connection with such a profane expression?" "I mean," said the clergyman, "that when I came from the far West, my bishop told me to put down on my subscription book every subscription I should receive, however small. [Laughter and applause.] I have simply obeyed his directions." "Very well, sir," said the merchant, "you have got the better of me this time. I am willing to pay for this bit of humor,"

and he offered the clergyman twenty-five dollars to erase
the objectionable subscription. "No, indeed," said the
clergyman, "that subscription is worth a great deal more
than twenty-five dollars." [Great laughter.] But to make
a long story short, the end of it was—and I tell the story to
illustrate the generosity of merchants in all matters of benevolence—the merchant who had welcomed the agent
with such profanity, handed him a check for two hundred
and fifty dollars. [Applause.]

This is an illustration, so far as I know them, of the
habits of the class to which you belong, and to which it is
the pride of my life that I was once privileged for a short
time to belong.

What is a merchant, unless he undertakes to exert upon
the community, through his calling, just such an influence
for good as your library undertakes to bear upon it!
What is the merchant, in other words, without the advantages of culture? What but a mere accumulator, who,
when he comes to the end of his busy and engrossed life,
and dies out of it, ceases to be of interest to the world, save
as his effects create an interest—so that the world forgets
the man in merely asking the gross and material question
—"What did he leave behind him?" On the contrary,
the merchant whose mind has been enlightened and elevated and enlarged by culture, who has learned to love letters, and through them to think of something else than
mere accumulation—he becomes the large-hearted bene-
factor in every good work. He founds the noble institutions of charity, and of literature, and of benevolence which
are destined one day to be the glory of this great commercial city, and keep potent, as I believe can be done in
scarcely any other way, the enriching and ennobling influences of the institution which you represent. [Applause.]

I thank you, Mr. Chairman, for the privilege of having
responded to the kindly sentiment which you have given

in behalf of the calling which I here, in part, represent. I desire no better alliance in the great work which the clergy are called upon to do in the City of New-York, than to be re-enforced by your merchants from day to day, and not only backed up by them, but, as I heard a clever parson say the other day, when making a strong appeal in behalf of a good cause—but "green-backed up" in behalf of all good works. [Applause.]

THE CHAIRMAN.—To almost every other toast given this evening, one response is enough, but so important a toast as that which I have just proposed, I think, will bear a few words from our venerable and much-esteemed friend, Dr. Adams.   [Applause.]

REV. DR. ADAMS.

I am very much obliged to you, Mr. President (although, as you yourself know, this is altogether unexpected upon my part), for the very kindly manner with which my name has been received, and this fresh reference to the profession of which I am permitted to be an humble representative.

In some parts of the world, and in many parts of the continent of Europe, men of action, of enterprise, men of the *world*, as we say, are in direct antagonism with churchmen or clergymen, not for the reason which I suppose none of them hold—that Christianity has no affinities to enterprise—but because, unhappily, in some parts of the world, those who represent the Church, have put themselves in opposition to liberty and to progress and to enterprise. Most fortunately, the reverse of that is true in our own country. And the very fact, that on an occasion like this, you have framed a sentiment in honor of the clergy, shows that in your apprehension, the clergy are the allies and the patrons of all that is liberal, and refined, and healthful in human society. [Applause.]

My eloquent friend and brother, Mr. Potter, knows that

we are accustomed to speak from texts. He has got
through, however, most happily, without one being given to
him; but if I were to fall upon a text (and I always want
some little plank to float upon when I am thrown upon the
water in this way), I should say that your very name, the
Mercantile Library Association—those two words, joined in
that connection—was a suggestive theme. There was a
time when the merchants were classed by themselves, just
as the clergy were classed by themselves; and the different
classes of society were distinguished by some peculiarity
in dress. The different classes then had rivalries and
antagonisms. We are all familiar—for books have been full
of them from the time of the old classics—with the pictures
representing the choices which men were to make in life.
It has been a very favorite mode of representing life to picture the world as a mart of commerce, where we have different objects to select from, and where the objects themselves are placed in rivalry or antagonism. It was supposed that it was absolutely necessary for a man in making
a choice, to confine himself to one particular class. Merchants, for instance, were not supposed to have any affinity
for literary pursuits, or to have any interest in books of any
kind, except such as are peculiar to counting-rooms, and
are called ledgers. But here you bring merchants and
books together in the Mercantile Library, which is a collection of books in the hands and for the use of merchants.
It is a libel that there is anything unreconcilable in these
pursuits; and the names that we might bring together, of
such men as Halleck, and Bryant, and Sprague—which are
just as familiar in the banking house, and on the exchange,
as they are in connection with the Muses—are a complete
refutation of the statement that these pursuits are irrecon-
cilable [Applause.]

I see sometimes on the doors of counting-rooms—"No
admittance except on business," but I do not believe that

that is the right thing for a merchant to put upon his fore-head. It was once, perhaps, but it is not now. I believe that there is something liberalizing in the pursuits of the merchant; and I believe also, that in the activity of a commercial metropolis there is everything favorable to in-tellectual development, if men did but know it. I think it is a great deal easier to give direction to a sparkling brook than it is to put motion into a dead, stagnant pool. To young men who are desirous of improving intellectually, and of making advance in everything that is noble, I should say, come to the city; stay not in the torpor and apathy of the country. For everything that is good, intellectually, morally, and spiritually, give me the life and the activity of the city. [Applause.]

It has been the attempt of philosophers—oftentimes in a somewhat facetious way—to give a definition of man as an animal, that would distinguish from other animals. Burke gave this definition: that man was an animal that *cooked his food;* to which a distinguished man replied that was hardly a correct definition, because there were some animals that subjected their food to a process somewhat similar to the culinary process. Adam Smith gave this definition: that "man was an animal that made bargains." You never knew one dog to exchange a bone with another dog. Now, for a man to devote himself, as his profession for life, to this matter of exchanging and bartering, and do it in a way that shall leave his name and his credit immacu-late, and still increase his material possessions, is a great art. Why, if my recollection is right, *mercor, mercari,* had some connection with old Mercury, and Mercury was the prince of thieves; and I think there is some affinity be-tween the two. There are some men who, in this matter of bartering, take undue advantages, which are not much to their honor or reputation. One of that class said once to Dr. Johnson—that hater of everything that was mean—" I

5

must live somehow." Johnson replied, "Sir, I deny your premises; it is not at all necessary that you should live somehow !" [Applause.] What is there that we should honor more than we do commercial honor? That word "credit," what a beautiful etymology it has—*credo*, "I believe him ;" "I trust him." That is the meaning of the word. How worthy of honor is that man who, in all his transactions with his fellow-men, in bartering, gaining, striving and acquiring, maintains a spotless honor and secures a credit such that one stroke of his pen would be recognized on every exchange in the world; a credit that would load ships in distant parts of the globe ! If there is not something in that that is noble and magnanimous— something that is chivalric—then I do not know who there is entitled to the name and honor of chivalry.

I have had a little intercourse with the merchants of New-York now during a pastorate of thirty-six years in this city ; and I heartily respond to everything that my friend, Dr. Potter has said. I never yet knew a good thing, a really good thing, that would commend itself to the sound judgment of men, and connected with morals or religion, for which I could not find a prompt and generous response to an appeal in its behalf from the merchants of the City of New-York. [Applause.] And at this time, when young men are making their plans for life, I do not know an opportunity more auspicious and more hopeful, for one who wishes to make his mark in the world, than a merchant who is truly magnanimous in his purposes, honorable in his intentions, correct in his dealings with his fellow-men, liberal in his pursuits, who knows that there are other books besides the ledger, and who reads them, and who is projecting (as men at this board have been, and as their successors, I know, will do) things which are to be permanent decorations of our city, in the interest of learning, philanthropy, and re-ligion. [Applause.]

THE CHAIRMAN: "The Clinton Hall Association—an enduring memorial of munificence on the part of our merchants: wisely bestowed and abundantly rewarded." [Applause.]

In regard to the person whom I intend to call upon to respond to this toast, I am a good deal in the position of the boys who, seeing an old man who was noted for his profanity, and who had a load of stone upon his cart, pulled the tail-board out, and in going up hill, of course, the stones were all scattered. The boys ran up the hill, expecting to hear a volley of profanity from this old man at this mishap which had occurred. But when the old man saw what had occurred, he looked on very complacently and said: "There is no use; words cannot express my feelings on this occasion."

I know I speak the feeling of all of you when I say, in regard to our friend, Isaac H. Bailey, that no words are necessary in introducing him to you this evening. [Applause.]

MR. ISAAC H. BAILEY.

I feel it a great honor to be asked to respond in behalf of the merchants of New-York who contributed to the building up of the Mercantile Library Association—that roll of honor containing the names of men who in their lifetime have distinguished themselves by recognizing the literary wants of the young merchants of New-York. I am particularly happy in being here to-night, on the occasion of our fiftieth anniversary, and when, after having passed around the hat so often, we are at length in the position of respectable gentlemen of means and resources, who give dinner parties and ask no favors. [Laughter and applause.] I am entirely satisfied that we should never have organized this Association of the Alumni, if we had not been in that situation of perfect independence which made our guests entirely sure that they would not be called upon for contributions.

My friend, Mr. Camp, in wording this toast, I am happy to say, has not connected this Association with those religious and other benevolent institutions which throw out such broad hints to wealthy citizens that somebody will profit by their death, by printing upon their programme a form of bequest to the association which they represent, and thus throwing out a very unpleasant idea to those gentlemen—of whom there may be some here—who may be contemplating a retirement from life. [Laughter.]

It is a sad thought, and one that has always been suggestive of very unpleasant ideas to me, that a man should be regarded as more profitable when in his tomb than in his life time. Happily, we have around us those who have distinguished themselves in their life time, during their mature years, and while they were in the full glow of health, by remembering the literary necessities of their fellows, and contributing most nobly to them. When we have our Stewarts, our Coopers, our Dodges in our midst, we need not look for the prosperity of our institutions in obituary notices. [Applause.]

I have a very pleasant memory of my connection with the Library Association in its earlier days, and I remember (and perhaps some of you are also sufficiently aged to remember), that when I came to the City of New-York, many years ago, I intimated to my confidential friends, that there was one round upon the ladder of fame to which I wished to aspire—and that was the presidency of the Mercantile Library Association. [Laughter.] It cost me several weary years of toiling ambition to attain that proud height, but having attained it, I assure you that the measure of my ambition was full; and I have since looked with sympathizing pity upon those who were struggling for that proud position. [Laughter and applause.] I am entirely willing that my honors should end with the distinguished office which I held then. Although I must confess, that not being gifted with foresight to see what would come, I did not, when I was president of the Mercantile Library Association, and looked over the figures of my annual report, which presented an aggregate of ten thousand per year of income, ever contemplate that I should witness the period (and perhaps I should not if I had not advanced to a serene old age), [great laughter,] when its resources would be fifty thousand dollars per year, and its increase of books twelve thousand volumes annually. I expect on the arrival of our one hundredth celebration, to be here [renewed laughter,] and congratulate you upon the realization of the dreams of our president—and all obtained out of that sinking fund which the Trustees of the Clinton Hall Association hold for the benefit of the Mercantile Library. [Applause and laughter.]

It is the custom, I believe, of every man who responds to a sentiment, to ignore the particular subject to which he is asked to respond; and I believe that I have been faithful to that part of the programme, and yet I would like to say, in behalf of this Clinton Hall Association, one single word ; that, having been created out of and being the outgrowth of the Mercantile Library Association, having been, in fact, elected the guardian of that Association, it has found itself the guardian of a very healthy and a very wholesome ward, which has occasioned little trouble, and which continues to thrive by the aid of its excellent guardianship. I am pleased in being able to state that in all the annual reports of the Mercantile Library Association which I have read, since the year 1841, there has been one very prosaic and yet very interesting sentence, and that is, " The Library is free from debt." Such a remarkable ambition has been presented among its officers to bring that sentence into each annual report, that I remember, on one occasion, when I was asking a president how he was going to state the fact to be in that respect, and whether he was going to give us our grand old sentence, " The Library is free from debt," he replied, " Yes ; we will report that, if we have to borrow the money." [Applause.]

Gentlemen, I have been favored by your Chairman with a telegraphic message, received to-day by the cable, from a former friend of the Association, now somewhat lukewarm with regard to all American institutions, but who, neverthe-less, has been very eminent in literature :

" Well, you have succeeded. Somebody is at the head of the heap. See what you can make of him. I have no faith in America, and no faith in fools.

" Yours respectfully,   T. CARLYLE."

But, gentlemen, I have the pleasure of stating to you that there is a liberal Member of Parliament here to-night who has faith in America, who has faith in ideas, and who is thoroughly *up* to our American institutions. I am going to ask you, with the permission of the chair to join with me in drinking the health of Mr. Mundella. [Applause.]

MR. A. J. MUNDELLA (who was greeted with cheers), said :

Mr. CHAIRMAN and GENTLEMEN—The Vice-President has proposed a very irregular toast, and one, indeed, for which I am entirely unprepared, but for which I must at least thank you from the bottom of my heart. I hope the kindly sentiments he uttered with respect to me, had more foundation in fact than had the cable message which he has read. [Laughter.] I trust that my countryman, Carlyle, although he does say some rude things, has not been guilty of sending such a message as that. [Applause and laughter.] At any rate, I can safely say that few things have pleased me more since I have been among you than to see the results of your great struggle, your recent war. My friend, Major-General McDowell, has made some very useful reflections on the real calamity which wars generally bring upon a nation; and he almost proved to my mind that, although he is a good soldier, he is a better Christian, and is somewhat in doubt, in his own conscience, of the use of his profession. But there have been few wars —none that I can remember—that show such useful results as yours has done. [Applause.] I think it one of the most gratifying features that I have ever witnessed, and one that I never witness without a great deal of admiration— that the negro, who we said was not a man and a brother (and as to whom I confess I brought with me to this country some of my English prejudices, although I have long been an emancipationist), has, after all, distinguished himself in this country, by an industry and by orderly habits, which not all the white men on our side of the globe display. [Applause.]

Whenever my countrymen return from America, they always speak of its splendid hospitality. I, too, shall have to sing the same song when I return. I can hardly thank Americans sufficiently for the kindly welcome which I have received; for I came among them a few months ago almost an entire stranger, yet everywhere have been received with the kindest welcome, to which no merits of mine entitle me.

I feel, as I know you feel, that we are all of one stock; and that there ought to be no dividing lines between us. [Applause.] It is true that I am a "liberal member of Parliament," as has been stated; but that phrase means something that you in this country have hardly yet come to realize. We represent the people of England—the men who were your allies throughout your great struggle; the men who stood by you in spite of poverty, and famine and suffering; and who were always true to you, notwithstanding the inducements and allurements presented to them to be the contrary.   [Applause.]

I am myself a large employer of labor (my trade was the custom trade), and I saw my workmen suffering for years in consequence of your war.   I never found a man among them—and I tried them again and again—who would say one word for the South.   Notwithstanding all they had to undergo, nothing could induce them to be untrue to their faith in your principles.   [Cheers.]

There has been a great revolution in England, although it has been a revolution without bloodshed.   The people have been permitted to share the political power.   Two hundred new and "liberal" members of Parliament were recently elected.   The members of the aristocratic party did not dare to meet that Parliament, but resigned before it was called together; and we have now in our government such men as no government in England has ever had before, and among them, and foremost, Gladstone, Bright, Forster, the Duke of Argyll.   Tradesmen and peers are now working side by side for the amelioration and emancipation of their country.   [Cheers.]

I must confess that, although you treat me so well as an individual, I cannot but perceive that you do not cherish the same kindly feeling towards my country.   It would be idle in me to attempt to disguise that there are grounds of discontent and disagreement between your country and mine.   But I cannot believe, I will not believe—and everything that I have seen and heard compels me to the contrary—that the sentiments which I find reported in the morning papers as the expression of an honorable member of your national legislature (General Butler) are the sentiments of the people of America.   I do not believe that you desire the humiliation of my country, or that you desire to go to war with it.   I believe that such a catastrophe would be one of the greatest that could afflict mankind. I may say, as one who was and is sincerely and staunchly your friend, that in whatever was done, or neglected to be done, whereby you were wronged, my countrymen are prepared to do you right, to the uttermost farthing. [Cheers.]

I cannot believe, I will not believe, that the intelligent citizens of this great continent desire to throw back the march of progress in my country by inflicting upon the millions of newly enfranchised workmen of England the horrors of an internecine war. I do not believe that such is the real sentiment of the people of this country. And I will say further, that the English people rejoice in your prosperity; we glory in your success; we do not envy it; we feel it as reflecting pride and satisfaction upon our own country. I believe in all I have heard to-night as to what may be your future. You cannot realize what your future will be. I sincerely trust that all your hopes and aspirations may be realized. When I presented myself to my constituency, in opposition to the man whose words rankle deepest in your bosoms, I appealed to them on the ground that our natural allies were the men who spoke our own tongue, and were our own kindred. Their appreciation of these sentiments is shown by the fact of my election over one of the ablest men of my country, by a majority of thousands.

I trust God will prevent any such misfortune to the people of both sides of the Atlantic, as I see foreshadowed in the article in this morning's papers. I say that any man, either on our side, or on yours, who desires to foment a war between people speaking the same language, trusting in the same Bible, having the same authors and traditions, and the same sentiments and aspirations, for the mere purpose of securing a political triumph, is guilty of the greatest crime under heaven! I trust you will forgive me for speaking thus earnestly. I hope to live to see the day when the whole English-speaking race will be confederated in one great bond of union; and if ever we do see that day, it will put an end to war and bloodshed throughout the world. [Long continued applause.]

THE CHAIRMAN.—Our last regular toast of the evening, is one with which you will all cordially sympathise:

"Woman—the only privileged class in our land; her rule is not disputed, because she derives her power from the consent of the governed."

We have with us an ex-Lieutenant-Governor of the State of New-York, who will respond to this toast—the Hon. Lyman Tremaine.

MR. TREMAINE.

.GENTLEMEN—Your chairman has called upon me, a comparative stranger to the merchants of New-York, and a non-resident of the city, to respond to the toast in honor of woman. If you were upon the witness stand, I should be inclined to ask you a question, and that would be in the language of Artemus Ward, in his address to the sixteen widows of a deceased Mormon, who were all making love to him at once, as he was about to leave Utah,—"Why is this thus?" [Laughter.] I suppose the answer of the chairman would be that, the subject he has given me is so very excellent in itself, and that its intrinsic beauty and purity are such, that it requires no ornamentation or embellishment, and therefore may be entrusted to the most ordinary speaker.

The subject that is given me reminds me of the story of a country horse jockey who was trying to sell a span of horses (one black and one bay) to a wealthy city customer, who spent his whole time in enlarging upon the excellent qualities of the bay, while the purchaser thought that the black horse was altogether the better of the two; and he said to the jockey: "Why is it that you are talking all the time about this bay horse, when the black horse seems to me to be the better?" "Ah," said the jockey, "the other horse will speak for himself." So it is with woman.

The Alpha and the Omega of the sentiment which I would advance with respect to this subject is simply this: that woman is the highest, the noblest, the holiest blessing that a kind Providence has ever vouchsafed to man. Some musty, fusty, crusty old bachelor might be disposed to take issue with me as to this, and to say that Eve was the first to introduce sin into the world. (A laugh.) Now, I have a great respect for the general opinions of mankind, yet I doubt if old Mother Eve has not been more sinned against than sinning. It is very certain that the Book says that she was herself first beguiled by the serpent, and of course *he* belonged to the masculine race. (Laughter.) I think the Bible also teaches us that when Eve sinned, it was for the benefit of her lord, Adam, and that she desired to elevate him to the dignity of a God, where he would know good from evil. But if you should see, as I have, the last and crowning work from the chisel of Hiram Powers, in his study at Florence, the magnificent statue of Eve, representing her at the moment when she says to the Lord, "The serpent beguiled me, and I did eat," and should notice the expression of sweet penitence and humility that he has so successfully infused into the marble, I am sure you would be disposed to pardon Eve, or that any resentment you might feel would be displaced by sympathy and pity. But if Eve sinned, I think the debt was more than paid when another woman gave us the Saviour, whereby Heaven and eternal happiness were opened to us.

Woman's influence is always on the right side; and she is the conservative force of humanity. This is acknowledged everywhere. What woman on earth has been more honored than the sovereign of the distingushed Member of Parliament who has addressed us to-night, [applause]—the model